Life in the Slow Lane

A Desert Tortoise Tale

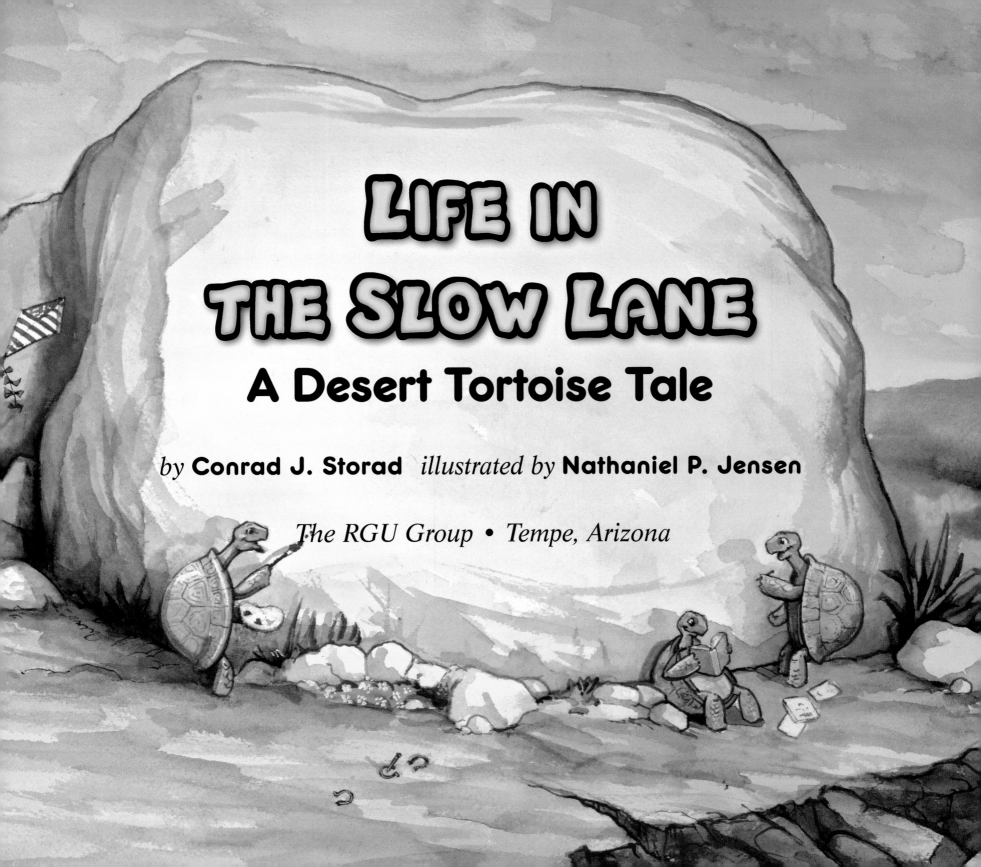

LIFE IN THE SLOW LANE
A Desert Tortoise Tale

by **Conrad J. Storad**   illustrated by **Nathaniel P. Jensen**

The RGU Group • *Tempe, Arizona*

The illustrations were rendered in watercolor on Arches paper
The text type was set in Life
The display type was set in Chlorinar and Frankfurter
Composed in the United States of America
Graphic layout by Adriana Patricia De La Roche

Printed in Singapore

First impression

Library of Congress Catalog Number: 2004099767

ISBN 10: 1-891795-07-4 —Hardcover
ISBN 13: 978-1-891795-07-7 —Hardcover

The RGU Group
www.theRGUgroup.com

11 10 9 8 7 6 5 4 3 2 (hc)

To Ryan, my nephew, and Taylor,
my niece. Stop. Look. Listen.
Enjoy the world's beauty and
share it with others.
— Uncle Top

To my wonderful wife, Cassandra
and my amazing son, Mason
— N.J.

It's life in the slow lane
The slow life for me!
The tortoise's way
Is the best way to be!

Young Shelly the Tortoise
Was singing one day
She went up to her Grandpa
To hear what he'd say:

"Come closer, dear Shelly,
I'll tell you a tale
Of our life in the desert
With cactus and quail.

"Our family's old
Listen close, now, my dear -
We've lived on this planet
For millions of years.

"We come from old stock
We have friends by the dozens -
And here's a surprise:
Crocodiles are your cousins!

"We eat leaves and grasses
Prickly cactus and flowers.
We always need water.
We can store it for hours!

"Our hind feet are thick
Kind of stubby and fat.
We're not built for racing
No doubt about that!

"Jackrabbits are speedy
Just look at them run!
A tortoise just thinks
Moving slowly's more fun.

"Wild hummingbirds hover
They dart and they scurry.
A tortoise just asks,
'Why on Earth should I hurry?'

It's life in the slow lane
The slow life for me!
The tortoise's way
Is the best way to be!

"Our front legs for digging
Are flat, wide and strong.
We dig dens and burrows
They're deep and they're long.

"We return to these burrows -
That's where we can hide.
When predators hunt us
We're safely inside.

"We're built for protection
With a strong bony shell.
We tuck head and tail in
And our four feet as well.

"Then nothing can hurt us!
We're tucked in for hours.
When the danger is gone
We come out to eat flowers.

"We can live to be sixty,"
Shelly's old Grandpa said.
"Some can live to a hundred
Some die young instead.

"Our desert is changing -
It's people, you know!
They like to move quickly.
They rarely go slow.

"They build homes and highways
They need lots of room.
But tortoises worry
Are we facing our doom?

"Let's try to convince them
The fast lane is wrong!
Remember the tortoise
And join in our song:

"Oh — It's life in the slow lane
The slow life for me!
The tortoise's way
Is the best way to be!"

DESERT TORTOISE
(Gopherus agassizi)

Size: *9 to 14 inches long; up to 11 pounds.*

Lifespan: *60 to 80 years or more.*

Diet: *Grasses, fleshy cactus pads, juicy cactus blossoms.*

Color: *Shell is tan to dark brown with yellowish plates; Head and legs are reddish brown.*

Range: *Mojave and Sonoran deserts of southeastern California; southern Nevada; western and south-central Arizona; southwestern Utah; Sonora and northern Sinaloa, Mexico*

Predators: *Ravens, roadrunners, hawks, coyotes, bobcats, kit foxes*

K eep your eyes open when you take a hike in Southwestern deserts. If you are lucky, you just might get to see a living relative of the dinosaurs. The desert tortoise is a distant cousin to those mighty prehistoric reptiles. It is also related to alligators and crocodiles. The desert tortoise is a member of a group of animals that have been on Earth for more than 200 million years.

But what about turtles? Is the tortoise a turtle, or is the turtle a tortoise? Actually, tortoise is the name scientists give to turtles that live on dry land. (Most turtles live in the water.) Tortoises like to drink water and bathe in it when they get a chance. There are 40 different kinds of tortoises living in the world today, and more than 260 different kinds of turtles.

In the Sonoran Desert of Arizona and Mexico, tortoises dig shelters in the loose gravel of arroyos or along rocky, boulder-strewn hillsides called bajadas. In the Mojave Desert of California and Nevada, tortoises like to dig deep burrows in flatter, rocky areas filled with creosote and other desert shrubs. The burrows provide a cool shelter from the harsh desert sun and protect them from hungry predators.

At dinner time, it is plants only for the desert tortoise. Their sharp, serrated jaws look a lot like the blade of a bread knife. The jaws are perfect for shredding tough grass and thick, pulpy cactus pads and blossoms.

Desert tortoises move slowly. When danger is near, they pull their head and legs inside the safety of their hard shell.

A tortoise shell can enclose the animal's entire body. It is made of two layers. The hard upper layer is called the carapace. The bottom layer is called the plastron. The outer layer of the carapace is formed by plates called scutes. Scutes are made of material much like your fingernail. The inner layer consists of curved plates made of bone. The shell also provides shade. The tortoise can store a month's supply of water in sacs under its shell.

The desert can be a very dangerous place to live. Every summer, baby tortoises hatch from eggs the size of Ping-Pong balls. Gila monsters and many kinds of snakes love to eat tortoise eggs, if they can find the nest. Tortoise hatchlings themselves are only about the size of silver dollars. It takes at least five years for the desert tortoise's shell to grow hard enough to protect it from hungry enemies.

The raven is the number one predator. Roadrunners, red-tailed hawks, coyotes, bobcats, skunks, and the bushy-tailed kit fox would also gladly eat a young tortoise. With so many creatures hunting the hatchlings, only two or three of every 100 will survive to become an adult. But if a desert tortoise can survive the first five years, it can live to be 100 years old or more.

Some Words to Learn

arroyo: (ah-ROY-oh) — A water channel found in desert areas. Arroyos are dry for most of the year. But they can fill quickly with water during a summer rain storm.

bajada: (bah-HAH-dah) — In desert areas, the gentle slope located between a valley floor and the steep upper parts of a canyon or mountain. A bajada is formed by the soil, loose gravel, and rocks that erode from the upper parts of the mountain or canyon.

burrow: (BUR-oh) — A hole or tunnel in the ground dug by a desert tortoise or other animal for use as home, nest, or shelter.

carapace: (KAR-ah-payss) — The upper shell of a tortoise or turtle.

creosote: (KREE-uh-soht) — A common desert shrub. The name refers to the plant's smell. When they get wet, the leaves of the creosote bush have a strong tar-like odor.

plastron: (PLASS-tron) — The bottom shell of a desert tortoise or turtle.

predator: (PRED-a-tohr) — An animal that hunts and eats other animals.

scutes: (SKOOTZ) — Plates made of tough material called keratin. Keratin is much like the material that forms human fingernails. Scutes cover the outer surface of a desert tortoise shell.

serrated: (seh-RAY-ted) — Notched or toothed on the edge. Saws and bread knives have sharp serrated edges that make cutting easy. A tortoise's serrated jaw helps it to shred and eat tough desert plants.

Author's Note

The Mojave and Sonoran deserts stretch across large portions of the American Southwest. These dry, rugged, beautiful lands are home to some of the most interesting animals in North America, including the desert tortoise. But they are not as remote as they used to be. People are moving to desert areas in greater numbers than ever before. With them come farms, canals, houses, schools, highways, and shopping centers. Each new development chips away at natural habitats once home only to desert creatures and plants.

The desert tortoise has been around for millions of years. But it is getting harder for this amazing animal to live a full life. In the Mojave Desert of California and Nevada, the tortoise population is considered "threatened" according to the federal Endangered Species Act. Tortoises in Arizona's Sonoran Desert may soon join the list. Even though the desert tortoise is protected by law, we need to respect the desert tortoise and the environment in which it lives. Only then can we be certain that others, now and in the future, will have a chance to appreciate this remarkable creature.

— Conrad J. Storad

CONRAD J. STORAD grew up in Barberton, Ohio. He has lived in the Sonoran Desert since 1982, when he began graduate school at Arizona State University. Currently, Storad is the editor of the national award-winning *ASU Research Magazine*, and is the founding editor of *Chain Reaction*, ASU's science magazine for young readers. He is the author of 17 books for children, including *Don't Call Me Pig! A Javelina Story*, and *Lizards for Lunch, A Roadrunner's Tale*. *Don't Ever Cross That Road! An Armadillo Story* is one of eight books nominated for the 2006 Arizona Young Reader Award.

In 2001, the Arizona Library Association and Libraries, Limited honored Storad with the Judy Goddard Award as Arizona's Children's Author of the Year. He is also a member the ASU Walter Cronkite School of Journalism's Hall of Fame. When he is not working, Conrad enjoys hiking and exploring the wilds of the Southwest with his wife, Laurie.

NATHANIEL P. JENSEN loved to draw when he was a little boy. He always said he wanted to be an artist when he grew up, but he never wanted to do it for a living. Still, since graduating from the University of Texas in 1991 he's done nothing *but* work for a living as an artist. He's created massive murals and oil paintings, developed animated movies and music videos, and designed and illustrated everything from brochures to books. (Visit him on www.natespace.com to learn more.)

Nathan is the illustrator of *Don't Ever Cross That Road! An Armadillo Story*, also by Conrad Storad. He lives in Austin, Texas, with his wife, Cassandra, and their young son Mason, who already inspires future projects.